WINTER FUN

Written by Rita Schlachter
Illustrated by Susan Swan

Troll Associates

Library of Congress Cataloging in Publication Data

Schlachter, Rita.
Winter fun.

Summary: Turtle longs for the joys of June until Rabbit introduces him to the fun of February.
[1. Winter—Fiction. 2. Turtles—Fiction. 3. Rabbits—Fiction] I. Swan, Susan Elizabeth, ill.
II. Title.
PZ7.S34647Wi 1986 [E] 85-14008
ISBN 0-8167-0584-4 (lib. bdg.)
ISBN 0-8167-0585-2 (pbk.)

Printed in the United States of America

10 9 8 7

WINTER FUN

It was February. Cold, wet snowflakes drifted to the ground. Turtle shivered inside his shell. He was looking at the calendar on the wall. The word FEBRUARY was on the top of the page.

There were twenty-eight squares on the page. Each square stood for one day in February. A red X was marked in the fifth square because it was the fifth day in February. There were twenty-three days left in that month.

Turtle looked at the picture on the calendar. The ground was covered with snow. A turtle was sliding down the hill on his shell, while two bunnies made a snowman.

Turtle turned the pages of the calendar. He stopped when the page read JUNE. In June the sun was out, and the air was warm.

Turtle wanted it to be June so he left the June page on the calendar. Then he went to the window to watch for the sun to come out and the air to feel warm.

Turtle waited and waited. The calendar read JUNE, but the snow kept falling. It was still February.

Between the falling snowflakes, Turtle saw Rabbit hopping over the hill, his long ears flopping up and down. The snow always made his ears droop. In the next minute, Rabbit hopped into Turtle's house.

“Were you waiting for me?”
asked Rabbit.
“No,” said Turtle. “I was
waiting for June.”

"It's February," said Rabbit.
"You'll be waiting a long time."
"No, I won't," said Turtle.
"Look at the calendar, it will be warm soon."

"Turning the calendar to June won't make it warm," said Rabbit.

"I hate cold weather," said Turtle. "There's nothing to do. When it's snowing we can't go on a picnic."

"Sure we can," said Rabbit.

"Can we take potato salad and lemonade and watermelon?" asked Turtle.
"No. We'll take hot chocolate and soup," said Rabbit.

Turtle and Rabbit packed the picnic basket. There was a jug of hot chocolate, a thermos of soup, cups, napkins, and a tablecloth. Turtle snuck in a few chocolate-chip cookies for dessert, when Rabbit wasn't looking.

Turtle put on his knitted hat
and his turtleneck sweater. Then
the two friends trudged through
the snow to their favorite picnic
place. It had stopped snowing.
Rabbit's ears were not drooping
as much now.

Turtle spread the tablecloth over the snow, while Rabbit poured the soup and hot chocolate into the cups.

"This is fun," said Turtle.
Then he looked at the tablecloth.
He looked at the snow.

"On winter picnics there are no
ants to pester us," said Turtle.
He looked in the air.
"And there are no bees to buzz
around our ears."

Turtle enjoyed the rest of his lunch. Then he surprised Rabbit with the chocolate-chip cookies.

Cookies

Turtle sat in the snow. He brushed some of the snow away so he could see the road.

"This is where I roller-skate in the summer," said Turtle. "I can't roller-skate in the snow. The snow keeps me from having fun."

Then Turtle walked to the pond. It was covered with ice. Turtle jumped up and down in the snow and shouted, "The pond is ruined! I can't swim, I can't roller-skate. February is no fun."

"We can't roller-skate in the snow, but the ice didn't ruin the pond," said Rabbit. "Instead of roller-skating, we can ice-skate. Watch me!"

Rabbit sailed across the ice. He twirled around and around, faster and faster.

Turtle decided to try. He put one foot on the ice. Very carefully, he put the other foot on the ice. Then he gave himself a little push.

Turtle slid slowly across the pond until he bumped into Rabbit and fell on his back. Turtle slid to the end of the pond on his shell.

Rabbit skated over to his friend.
He gave Turtle a hard push.
Laughing, Turtle sailed across
the pond on his shell.
"Now you can skate without
falling down," said Rabbit.

On the way home Turtle stopped by a large oak tree. He brushed the snow away from around the roots of the tree. "In June, wild strawberries grew here," said Turtle. "I would stop on my way home from the pond and pick them for my lunch."

Rabbit twitched his nose, but didn't answer.

"And look!" said Turtle. "My grill is buried under the snow. Now we can't roast marshmallows after supper."

"But we can roast marshmallows in the fireplace," said Rabbit.

And that is just what they did.

Afterwards, Turtle got up and went straight to the calendar on the wall. It still read JUNE.

"We went on a picnic with good things to eat," said Turtle. "We went ice-skating instead of roller-skating. We roasted marshmallows inside instead of outside."

June

Turtle turned the pages of the
calendar back to February.
"We had a nice day. February's
not so bad after all!"